Taking Delilah

L.T. Ryan

PUBLISHED BY:

Liquid Mind Media

Copyright © 2012

All rights reserved.

No part of this publication may be copied, reproduced in any format, by any means, electronic or otherwise, without prior consent from the copyright owner and publisher of this book.

This is a work of fiction. All characters, names, places and events are the product of the author's imagination or used fictitiously.

The blue and rust colored Chevy Nova clunked and banged to a stop on the sandy shoulder of highway 128.

"Shit. You've got to be kidding me." Delilah Barrow slammed her fist into the dashboard.

"Out of gas," Dean said. "Sorry, babe. Thought I could get us there." He took his hat off, wiped the sweat from his brow and ran his hands through his short brown hair.

Delilah rubbed the knuckles on her right hand, still sore from her attempt at knocking out the Nova. "I'm so screwed. They are going to fire me if I'm late today."

Dean shifted forward and reached into his back pocket to pull out his cell phone. "Give them a call. They'll give you a break." He brushed her long blond hair out of her face and leaned in for a kiss.

She pushed him back with one hand and flipped the phone open. "For real?" She flung the phone at his crotch. "No service out here." She sat back in the seat, crossed her arms and bit her bottom lip.

"There's a gas station not far from here. Give me the number and I'll call after I get some gas."

The desert landscape expanded before her. The sun was deep in the western sky, close to setting for the evening. Entranced by the scenery, she flinched when Dean opened her door.

"Will you be okay while I'm gone?"

Her legs swung out of the car and she planted her feet in the sand that covered the road shoulder. "Can't I go with you?"

"I'm planning on running. Think you can keep up?"

Delilah fumbled through her purse and pulled out a cigarette. "Screw that. I'll wait here."

Dean took his shirt off and tossed it at her. It was over one hundred degrees and sweat ran down his underdeveloped chest and got caught in his small collection of belly hair. Delilah smiled. He wasn't a body builder, but he turned her on.

"Back in twenty or thirty minutes, D." He sprinted off.

She got out of the car and leaned against the door. Dean disappeared into mirage of concrete and desert. She climbed on top of the car and leaned back against the windshield, one hand behind her head, the other fingering her cigarette. The cigarette burned down and she flicked it onto the highway. Then she closed her eyes and hummed an old country song from her youth.

Delilah woke to the sound of screeching car tires. According to her watch she had been asleep for close to 20 minutes. She sat up and looked around. Dean was nowhere to be seen.

The white Ford station wagon backed up and stopped next to her. There was a woman in the passenger seat. She looked young, but Delilah guessed that she was in her mid-thirties judging by the grey her hair that had accumulated around her temples. A man leaned across the woman and asked, "Car troubles?"

Why did people always have to state the obvious? She resisted the urge to make a smart ass remark. "Yeah, out of gas. My boyfriend left about twenty minutes ago to get some."

"Gas station is more than three miles from here, darling. Why don't you get in? We'll run you up the road." He gestured to the back seat.

Delilah wasn't sure. She had never hitched a ride. She leaned over and looked in the backseat. There was a little boy strapped into a car seat and a Jack Russell terrier panting away. Delilah looked at the woman in the front seat. She sat motionless, expressionless, just staring ahead. Delilah figured that the woman was pissed off her husband had stopped to help an attractive young woman rather than get her home or wherever it was they were going.

"It'll be dark soon," the man said. "It's not safe to be out here after dark. You don't know who is on the road."

Delilah studied him. If he were alone, there was no way she would get in the car with him. She didn't see him as a threat though. He looked harmless. He had a nice smile and calming presence. A little padding around the midsection, but other than that he had nice features. He looked like a regular guy. A nice, regular, helpful guy.

"Okay. Thank you." She got in the backseat.

A few minutes later Delilah spotted Dean. She reached in between the man and his wife and pointed at the silhouette on the side of the road. "That's him."

The car pulled over to the side next to Dean who was walking, not running, just like Delilah figured he'd be.

She leaned over the little blond haired boy and stuck her head out the window. "Get in loser."

Dean stopped walking when he saw Delilah. He put his hands on his knees in an attempt to catch his breath and then joined her in the backseat. "Thanks," he said to the driver. He turned to face Delilah. "Gas station's further away than I thought it would be."

The driver turned his head back toward them. "Where you headed?"

"Eunice," Delilah responded. "Supposed to work tonight. Hopefully they don't fire me for being late."

"We can take you to Eunice," the man said.

"That's okay, sir," Dean said. "Just need to get some gas and get back to the car."

"Actually," Delilah said. "I might be able to make it on time if we go straight to the restaurant."

Dean looked at her like she was crazy.

She smiled and winked at him.

She knew he couldn't resist her blue eyes and full lips. "I guess that'll work." He looked down at his cell phone. The look on his face told her that there was still no signal.

"Hey, there's the gas station." Dean pointed out the window to his left. "Might as well get some now."

The driver paid no attention to them as he hummed along with the radio. The woman in the passenger seat looked to her left and opened her mouth to speak. The driver raised his right index finger at her and wagged it side to side. The woman slumped back in her seat and covered her mouth with her hand.

"Guess not then," Dean muttered as the car passed the gas station.

Delilah stared at the rear view mirror, studying the man driving the station wagon. He looked up and they locked eyes. A shiver went down her spine. It was unlike anything she had ever felt before. Was it fear? Panic? A premonition? Dean reached over and grabbed her hand and the feeling subsided. She brushed it off and leaned back into Dean's sweaty chest. He put his arm around her and kissed the side of her head. She let herself drift off to sleep again.

Delilah woke to the sound of Dean yelling to be heard above the rush of the wind. She opened her eyes and saw him pointing out the window to the left.

"Hey, Eunice is that way man."

The driver either didn't hear him or ignored him.

Delilah sat up and saw they were in the town of Jal. The small airport was coming up on the left. The driver had missed the turn. "Hey, mister. He's right. You missed the turn. That's the airport right there. Keep going this way and we'll be in Texas in a few minutes."

He looked at her in the rear view mirror and winked. "Just a slight detour, darling."

She leaned forward in between the front seats and smacked him on the shoulder. "No. Turn around or let us out."

He didn't acknowledge her.

She turned to the lady in the passenger seat. "Hey, what is wrong with your husband? Tell him to stop the car. Let us out."

The lady didn't speak. She looked at Delilah from the corner of her eye. Tears were starting to fall down the woman's cheek.

Delilah grabbed the man's arm and yelled in his ear. "Stop the car now."

He slammed on the breaks, the car screeched to a stop. He reached over and pulled Delilah by her hair, slamming her head into the dashboard. She heard a thud from the backseat and the sound of Dean crying out.

The driver let go of Delilah who scrambled to get herself turned around and in the back seat again.

Dean's face smacked the back of the driver's seat when the car stopped. Blood was dripping from his nose, his eyes watered. He swung blindly trying to catch the back of the man's head. He landed a punch in the middle of Delilah's back. She shrieked. He got a hand around the driver's neck.

The driver reached up with his left hand and grabbed Dean's wrist and began twisting it.

Dean's body was lifted up by the force on his wrist. The side of his head pressed into the roof. Once Dean's grip on the man's neck was released, the man reached under his seat and pulled out a gun. He pointed the gun at them. The woman in the front was crying, as was the little boy in the car seat.

"Now listen here," the driver said. "Any of you move and all four of you are dead. I'll run this car into a damn pole if I have to."

Dean pulled on the door handle. "Let us out of here man."

The driver cocked the gun and put it up to Delilah's forehead. "Maybe you didn't hear me right, son. I said any of you move and I'll fucking kill all four of you."

"Please just do what he says," the woman in the front seat pleaded.

"What the hell is going on here?" Dean asked. "Just let us go."

The driver looked beyond them out the back window and then got out of the car. Delilah shivered and broke down, tears streaming down her face. The gun was no longer at her, that was a relief. But now she had no idea what the man was going to do. The door next to Dean jerked open. The driver grabbed Dean's arm and yanked him out of the car. Dean let out a grunt as his head smacked the cracked asphalt.

Delilah looked over and saw his legs dragging along the ground. She swung her head around in time to see the trunk pop open. There was the distinct sound of Dean's body being dropped into it. The trunk lid slammed shut, seconds later the man stuck his head in the back door.

"You want to join him?"

Delilah shook her head.

"Then shut the hell up unless I say otherwise."

The air was full of the sounds of Dean's muffled screams and banging inside the trunk.

Delilah covered her face with her hands and cried.

Delilah wasn't sure how much time had passed. She drifted in and out of consciousness. She was there but not. Was it all a dream? Minutes flew by, and seconds stretched into hours. It was dark out and they were deep in the back country. No streetlights, no houses, no cars. She felt the car slow down and she made out the faint glow of a porch light in the distance.

The car bounced as it pulled into the driveway and slowed to a stop. The driver reached up and pressed a red button on a device attached to his visor. The garage door creaked and banged as it lifted up. A dim light flicked on, illuminating the empty garage.

"We're here."

"Where is *here*?" Delilah asked.

He caught her eye in the rear view mirror. "Your new home."

She bit her tongue and stared back at him while trying not to cry. She refused to let him see her scared.

He opened his door and stuck a foot out, then paused and looked over the seat at her. "Now, I'm going to get the bonehead out of the trunk. You move, he's dead." He pulled out his gun and tapped it against the headrest.

She looked around trying to figure out where they were and if anyone might be nearby. She closed her eyes and felt the car bounce up and down as the trunk opened and the man pulled Dean out. She heard Dean's body fell to the floor. *Was he dead?* Delilah started to panic, her breathing rapid and shallow.

"Where the hell are we?" Dean asked.

Delilah exhaled and wiped tears away from her cheek.

"Where the hell are we?" Dean asked again.

Delilah looked out the back window in time to see the driver strike Dean across his face with the butt of his gun. Dean staggered back, took a step toward the man, and then fell against the car. The driver grabbed him by his hair and dragged him to the corner of the garage where he pointed at the floor. Dean pushed himself up and rested on his knees.

"Open it," the driver said.

Dean reached down and pulled on a handle on the garage floor. A trap door opened. Dean crawled forward with his arms extended and pushed the trap door against the wall.

The driver motioned for Dean to go down the hole. Dean looked back at the car and tried to smile at Delilah, but he was barely able to move his mouth. The driver kicked him in the back and Dean lurched forward and fell into the hole.

The driver motioned to the car with his gun, pointing at the woman in the front seat. She undid her seat belt and stepped out of the car.

"Get your boy," the driver said.

She leaned in and unstrapped the little boy from the car seat, never making eye contact with Delilah. The driver motioned with his gun for her to go down the hole in the floor. She held the little boy tight to her chest and descended into the dark hole.

The driver pointed the gun at Delilah and motioned for her to get out of the car.

Her body refused to move. She hung her head and sat there, ignoring his command.

She felt the car shake when the driver slammed the trap door shut. She looked up and saw him lock it by sliding a metal pole through two iron u-bolts attached to the top of the door. He approached the car, his gun aimed at her head.

She lifted her arms and put her hands out in front of her. "Okay," she said. She backed out of the car. If he was mad enough to hit her it wouldn't be in the face.

He reached in, grabbed her by the hair and dragged to the corner of the garage. "On your knees facing that way." He pointed to the wall.

Delilah kneeled down. "You won't get away with this."

"Is that right?" The driver slid the pole out of the u-bolts and propped himself on it. "How do you figure that, darling?"

She cringed at the word darling. "Work will be looking for me. When they can't get a hold of me someone will stop by. My parents will call the cops. We drove through two towns, someone had to have seen us."

He threw his head back and laughed. "You really think anyone at Sid's Steakhouse gives a shit about you? They were ready to fire you."

She glanced back at him with a confused expression. *How did he know where she worked?*

"And your parents? Where are they? Not in that rusted old trailer you and your boyfriend live in."

Delilah tried to reply, but nothing came out when she opened her mouth.

"Here is how it will happen." He grabbed her hair and jerked her around to face him. "Your manager at work will figure you were a no show again and they'll just erase your name from the schedule. Maybe a couple of your co-workers will call to check in on you, but you weren't really that friendly with any of them."

Delilah's eyes darted around the garage. The only way out was blocked by the man and he clearly outweighed her by over a hundred pounds.

He noticed she fixed her gaze on the door to the house and he moved to the right to block her path. "And back to your parents. Come on, Delilah. How often do you speak to them? Once a month, maybe? They figure you're a lost cause."

Delilah shook her head. How did he know these things? Did she know him? No matter how hard she tried, she couldn't place him.

He knelt down in front of her reached out and tucked her hair behind her ear. "Don't worry. I'll take care of you."

"What? Who?" She couldn't find the words.

He laughed at her and dropped his arms, resting them on his knees.

Delilah seized the opportunity. She swung her arm, fist clenched, and struck him on the side of his face. He tumbled over and she scrambled to get to her feet. She shrieked as she planted her broken hand into the ground. At least one finger was broken by the impact with his jaw, maybe more. Her hand gave way and she fell forward, her face crashed into the concrete floor.

The man slid back against the wall and propped himself up. He rose to his feet and stood over her. "Big, big mistake, darling." He let out a grunting sound.

Delilah felt a flash of pain in the back of her head. Black spots littered her vision. Everything went black and she collapsed on the floor.

Delilah's head throbbed. Her face stuck to the cold concrete floor, glued in place by her own dry blood. She pushed her body up and peeled her face off the ground. The room was dimly lit. The walls were painted black. The air was cool and stunk of mildew.

Dean crawled over and helped her to her knees.

She stared into his brown eyes. "Where are we?"

He shrugged. "Wish I knew." He sat back against the wall and drew his knees to his chest. "One minute I'm walking along the road, the next I'm in some fucking dungeon." He buried his face into his hands.

Delilah leaned against him and put her arm around his back. "At least..."

"He's going to kill one of you."

The both looked up at the woman who had occupied the front passenger seat.

"That's what he does."

"How do you know?" Delilah asked.

She raised an eyebrow at Delilah. "Don't remember me?"

Delilah raised an eyebrow and studied her face. "Never seen you in my life."

"You sure about that?" the woman asked.

Delilah shrugged and held out her hands palms up.

"About a month ago, at Sid's Steakhouse. We sat next to one of your tables."

Delilah rolled her eyes. "I'm sorry, a lot of people have sat next to my tables."

"You tripped and spilled a drink all over your customer."

Delilah's face twisted as she remembered the incident. "Was that you?"

"No," the woman said. "Luke tripped you."

"Who?"

The woman pointed up. "Him," she mouthed without uttering a sound. "He got up to help you and you brushed him off. I knew then. I could see the look in his eyes. He glared every time you passed. Tried to get your attention a time or two. You ignored him."

"I don't understand. I'm here because..." she paused. "Because I ignored him at Sid's Steakhouse?" Despite the unsure tone of her voice, Delilah started to piece it together. She started picturing his face in different locations. At the bar at work. Walking through the trailer park. At the grocery store. She realized the reason why he looked so normal to her when he stopped to help. Everywhere she had been the last three weeks, he was there too.

The woman shifted to her knees, crawled over to Delilah and gave her a hug. "I'm sorry, sweetheart. I told him to leave you alone. He could do what he wanted with me. Leave the girl alone. I told him over and over."

"Why did he have to pick him up then?" Delilah pointed at Dean.

"Someone has to die," the woman replied.

Dean furrowed his brow at her. His nostrils flared. He lunged at the woman and placed his hands around her throat.

"Dean, no!" Delilah screamed. "Let her go, he might kill us if you hurt her. You don't know what he'll do." She pulled at Dean's hair and dug her long nails into his arm.

Dean looked at Delilah and let go of the woman. The woman scrambled to the other side of the room and fished around for something to defend herself with.

"Sorry," said Dean panting. He made his way to the corner, closed his eyes, and faked sleep.

Moments passed. "He's just scared," Delilah said.

"We all are," the woman said.

"The little boy, he's your son?"

The woman nodded.

"Where is he?"

"Luke keeps him upstairs. Tells him that I'm away at work."

"Are you scared he's going to hurt him?"

The woman licked her lips and swallowed hard. "I don't think he will." The look in her eyes betrayed her.

"How did you get here?" Delilah asked.

"He rescued us." The woman spit at hairs stuck to her lips. "We were at the Piggly Wiggly getting groceries. My old man was beating me. Stupid argument over ice cream. Always something stupid. But he took a swipe at the boy too."

Delilah shuffled across the floor to get closer to the woman.

"Luke came around the corner. Grabbed Gary's arm from behind as he took another swing at me." She lifted her arm into the air and then pulled back quickly to demonstrate. "Then Luke reached into his hand cart and pulled out a can of baked beans. He just went crazy. Slamming that can of beans over and over into Gary's head. By the time he was done, Gary was a lump of a man on the ground. Blood and baked beans covered his head and the floor." The woman giggled.

Delilah sat wide eyed. She didn't know whether to hug the woman or laugh along with her.

"So Luke picks up my son and grabs me by the arm. Drags me out of the store, into his car. I figure he's going to take me to the police. But he just kept driving." She looked over at the corner, at Dean. She said quietly, "Honest truth, I wanted to fuck him right then and there. I don't know that I'd ever been so turned on. When he drove past the police station I started to come onto him."

Delilah frowned at the woman. She was an attractive woman, one that most men would consider a prize catch. What kind of life did she have that she was drawn to these psychopaths?

"So we get here, he pulls into the garage. I get out of the car, run up to him, throw my arms around him, you know, kissed him." She looked down, her eyes watered. "He hugged me. Gentle at first. But then his grip tightened. I, I couldn't breathe." The woman looked up, tears streamed down her face. "Then he tossed me like a rag doll into the wall. Knocked me out cold. I woke up who knows when. Found myself chained to the wall here."

Delilah comforted the woman and stroked her long brown hair. "What's your name?"

"Misty."

"How long were you down here before he let you out, Misty?"

"No telling. But next time I saw him, he had Gary with him." She smiled and wiped her tears away.

For the first time, Delilah noticed that Misty was missing one of her front teeth, at the top of her mouth next to her incisor. "What happened?"

"He had me choose."

"Choose?"

"My freedom, or Gary's death."

"Sounds one in the same."

Misty shrugged. "He would let me go free. I could walk out. But it was on the condition that he kept my son. And that he would let Gary go five minutes after I left. He wouldn't intervene with anything that happened after that."

"So I'm guessing you chose Gary's death then."

She nodded. "It wasn't that simple though."

"How's that?"

Misty cleared her throat and leaned forward. "He made me do it."

A knot formed in the pit of Delilah's stomach as she sunk back against the wall.

"Get up," Luke yelled into the cellar.

Delilah shielded her eyes from the bright light. Why was it so bright? Was the garage door open? Could they make a break for it? If all three of them ran he would only be able to stop one of them.

Luke stood at the top of the wooden stairs. He pointed at Misty with his gun. "You first."

Misty crawled up the stairs. Luke pulled her up by her arm the last few stairs and tied her hands together with large zip ties.

He pointed the gun at Delilah, who followed Misty's path. He zip tied her hands together and then strung together a series of 5 zip ties to connect the women together at the elbow. *So much for running,* thought Delilah. The look Misty gave her said as much.

Dean scrambled to the stairs and climbed up. His head emerged from the cellar opening. Delilah cringed at the site of his beaten face.

Luke pushed Dean's head back down with the heel of his boot. "Not you cowboy, not yet." He grabbed a package of hot dogs and tossed them down to Dean. Then closed and locked the trap door.

As Luke led the women into the house, Delilah could hear the sound of Dean banging against the trap door. His muffled screams fading with every step she took.

Luke ordered the women to sit down at a table and he placed two cups of coffee and a plate of pancakes in front of them.

"Where's Jake?" Misty asked.

Luke pointed to the back of the house. "Watching TV." He whistled a tune from *Cats* as he brought butter and syrup to the table.

"I have to use the bathroom," Delilah said.

Luke grabbed a large knife from the counter and lowered it to his side, the tip of the blade pointing at Delilah.

She gasped, every muscle in her body froze. She didn't dare blink.

He walked over and cut the makeshift handcuffs connecting the two women. "You try anything," he paused to clear his throat, "and your boyfriend is dead."

Delilah returned to the table after washing up. Her coffee was cold. She spit it back into the cup.

"Sorry about that. Can't have you throwing a cup of scalding hot coffee at me."

The women finished their breakfast and Luke brought them back to the empty garage. He instructed to them to stand in the corner while he closed the garage door. The car was in the driveway. Against the wall were metal folding chairs and a matching table.

Delilah pictured herself as one of those pro wrestlers her and Dean watched on TV, smashing the metal folding chair into the back of Luke's head. Then she would pick him up, slam him into the table, and stand over him laughing as he lay amid the splintered particle board table.

Luke caught her grinning at him. "Don't go falling in love with me, Darling. You probably aren't going to like me that much in a few minutes." He grabbed three chairs and set them in a triangle shape. He made Delilah sit at one, Misty at the other. The chair in the middle was empty. He zip tied the women's legs to the chairs so they couldn't stand. At least not with any semblance of balance. If they tried to get up and run, they would fall.

Luke removed the pole that locked the trap door, lifted it and motioned for Dean to come out.

Dean shielded his head as he emerged from the hole in the floor, probably to protect himself from another boot to the head.

"Sit." Luke pointed to the empty chair.

Dean gave Delilah a concerned look as he passed her.

Luke followed and strapped Dean's legs to the chair. He walked behind him, grabbed Dean's arms, and then tied them behind his back. It was obvious he didn't want to take any chances with the young man.

Luke set up the table against the wall, ten feet in front of Dean. He hopped up on it and swung his dangling legs back and forth. He pointed at Misty and started saying, "Eeny, meeny, miny, moe." His finger moved between his prisoners with each word. "Catch a tiger by the toe. If he hollers, let him go, Eeny, meeny, miny, moe." His finger stopped on Dean. He paused long enough to look at all three of them individually. "My mom told me to pick the very best one," the word *one* was drawn out and he scanned his finger back and forth.

He pointed at Luke. "And you."

Then at Misty. "Are."

Then at Delilah. "It."

Delilah gasped. In her head she had planned his movements with the traditional version of the rhyme, *and you are not it.* She started to cry. He was going to kill her, she was sure of it.

Dean fought against his restraints. "Don't you fucking touch her." He got to his feet but lost his balanced and crashed hard, the side of his face smacking the concrete floor. He flailed around trying to lift himself up. It was pointless. He was like a fish on land.

Luke walked over and kicked him in the ribs. Then he stepped over Dean and opened up the door to the house. "Matty, come here buddy."

"Leave him alone," Misty yelled.

Luke ignored her. He picked Matty up and carried him over to the table. He directed his attention to Delilah.

"I don't want to die," Delilah pleaded through her sobbing.

Luke walked over to her and stroked her hair. "There, there. You aren't going to die."

"Really?"

"Yeah." He grabbed the back of her hair, pulled her head down, forced her to look up at him.

"But you are going to decide who will."

The room fell silent.

"What?" Delilah asked.

"It's your choice, darling." He returned to the table and picked up the little boy. "Here are your options Delilah." He licked his lips. "Either Matty here dies," he stopped and looked at Misty.

Misty screamed and frantically tried to free herself from her chair.

Luke walked over to Delilah and knelt down, placing the little boy's face right in front of hers. "Matty's life, or," he paused and looked over at Dean. "His life. No, no, wait that is too easy. Not his life. His testicles."

"What?" Delilah asked.

"You sonovabitch," Dean yelled.

Luke grabbed Delilah's jaw and put his face inches from hers. His hot breath invaded her mouth and nose. "It's your choice. You have 30 minutes."

"What happens after 30 minutes?"

"You all die."

The group sat in silence for the next 30 minutes. Delilah stared at the floor. Was it possible this was really happening? How did this small town girl find herself in this position?

Luke entered the garage carrying Matty on his hip. "Time's up, darling." He set Matty down and lifted Dean's chair off the ground.

Delilah looked up and met Luke's stare.

"Who's it going to be?" He patted the little boy on the head and pulled Dean's head back by his hair.

She looked at Dean and couldn't tell if he was angry, terrified, or both. Delilah opened her mouth to speak, but nothing came out.

Luke cocked his head to the side and pulled out his gun. He stuck the barrel on the top of the little boy's head. "Give me an answer or I'll start with him."

How could he be so calm?

Delilah glanced at Misty, who was in tears, head tucked into her chest. She shifted her gaze to Dean. He was slumped back in his chair, looking to the side. Was there really a choice? In the end they were all dead anyways. But she couldn't die knowing she condemned a little boy.

"Dean," she said.

"No, no, no," Dean shouted. "Please God no." His face was contorted, his final words interrupted by heavy sobs.

Luke put his gun away and picked up the little boy. "Very well," he said as he and Matty walked back into the house.

Twenty minutes passed. Dean shifted between whimpering and outbursts directed at all of them.

Misty looked like a zombie, her face pale and unflinching.

Delilah tried to cry, but there were no tears left. She wrestled with her decision, but she couldn't condemn that little boy to death. She went over every possible situation, but couldn't come up with anything or any way to get them out of here.

The door burst open and Luke stood there holding Matty in one arm and a bucket in the other. He grabbed a chair for Matty and set him in the corner with a portable DVD player and headphones.

"Why is he in here?" Misty asked.

"Insurance." He nodded and pointed at Delilah. "Just in case she doesn't go through with it."

"Go through with what?" Delilah asked.

"Oh, Delilah, did I leave that part out?" He threw his hands up in the air. "You are going to carry out the sentence."

Delilah's vision clouded over with black spots, she thought she was going to pass out. She leaned over and threw up. "Just kill me," she whispered.

"Nope, not part of the deal," Luke said. He was busy setting things on the table. There were restraints, a blowtorch, and a long knife. He unsheathed the knife and admired the sharp steel blade. He winked at Dean. "Ready?"

Dean sobbed. He said something, but it was unintelligible.

Delilah watched as Luke struck Dean in the head several times leaving him on the brink of unconsciousness. He dragged the chair over to the table, cut the zip ties, and then tossed her battered boyfriend onto the table. He placed Dean's hands and feet into the restraints and locked them in place. He started the blowtorch and heated up the knife, the blade had a faint orange glow. With the knife he cut Dean's remaining clothes off. With Dean naked on the table, Luke turned his attention to Delilah.

He reheated the blade and walked over to Delilah.

She sat defiant as he held the blade to her face. He slowly traced the tip of the blade down her cheek. She clenched her teeth, fighting back a scream. Why? Because fuck him, that's why.

"Just so you know how it feels," he said to her.

He cut her zip ties and led her to the table. She threw herself onto Dean's chest and kissed him. "I'm sorry," she said over and over.

Dean was semiconscious at this point. He told her he loved her and then his eyes rolled back in his head.

"Enough," Luke shouted. He grabbed Delilah by her hair and yanked her away from Dean.

Luke reignited the blowtorch and held the blade in the flame until it was bright red. He took Delilah's hand and placed the knife in it. "You'll want to be quick. It's going to be more painful when that knife cools off." He backed up with his gun aimed at her.

Delilah turned to face him and pointed the knife at him. Her hand trembled. She debated whether or not she should lunge at him. Could she make it? There was less than ten feet separating them. He would be able to get a shot off. Could she tolerate the searing pain of a bullet penetrating her and still make it to him? Would she be able to stab him with the knife? What if she missed? She hesitated too long.

Luke smiled and cocked the gun. "You'll never make it, darling." He kept backing up until he was next to Matty. "I can shoot him *and* you before you make it to me."

Delilah screamed and held the knife over her head.

"Do it now," Luke yelled. He grabbed the little boy and held him up by his neck with one hand. With his other hand he pointed the gun at the little boy's head.

Delilah spun and plunged the knife into Dean's abdomen. She held the knife still.

Dean screamed, his body jerked upward. He lifted his head, a betrayed look on his face as he stared at her holding the knife that was inside his body.

Tears streamed down her face. She pushed the knife deeper and ripped up toward his chest. His screams bounced off her ears, she just wanted him to die quickly and not suffer at the hands of the psychopath that held them captive.

Luke dropped Matty and rushed to the table. He knocked the knife out of Delilah's hand, picked her up by her neck and flung her into the garage door. "What did you do?" He stood over Dean, staring at his torn abdomen. "Dammit, you stupid girl. You've ruined my plan."

Delilah pulled herself up to her feet. She had a gash on her forehead, blood streamed down her face. "Fuck you. I'd rather see him dead than do that to him." She spit a mouthful of blood in Luke's direction.

Luke tapped the top of his head with his gun. He pointed it at Delilah, and then at Dean, then back at Delilah. He screamed and then fired four shots into the dying man on the table.

Dean's body was lifeless.

Delilah fell to her knees and covered her head with her hands. Everything was in slow motion, the noise drowned out. For a moment she thought she was the one who had been shot and was dying. She felt his hand on her head and everything sped up as Luke dragged her by her hair to the cellar. He dropped her on the floor. She saw Matty standing in the corner crying. She caught a glimpse of Misty who had her eyes clenched shut, face turned to the side. The door flung open and she was suspended mid-air, hovering over the cellar opening.

"Take one last look at him," Luke said as he carried her back to the table.

He lifted her over Dean's lifeless body. She reached out to touch his face but was spun around and again hovered over the dark hole leading to the cellar.

"Bitch," he said.

He let go. She felt weightless for a moment, then was greeted by the sensation of slamming into the concrete floor. Pain shot down her left arm, it broke on impact. She grimaced and listened as Luke went crazy in the garage.

"Leave him alone," Misty yelled.

"I'm sick of you two. Goddammit." Luke yelled like a beast.

Delilah heard two gunshots. She heard Misty scream and then say no over and over. Delilah cringed.

"He's just a little boy," Misty said in between heavy sobs.

Another gun shot. Then silence.

Footsteps above, closer and closer. Delilah lay as still as possible. She prayed that he would assume the fall killed her. She heard his labored breathing from above. The trap door slammed and she breathed a sigh of relief. She heard the sound of the car starting. It revved up and then faded away. Second passed. Seconds turned into minutes. She fought to remain conscious.

Tires squealed.

Boot steps. Getting closer and closer.

Click-clack.

Click-clack.

Click-clack.

The sound of the boot steps stopped. Delilah braced herself. The trap door swung open.

All at once Delilah heard the bang, the cellar lit up, and her back stung where the bullet entered her body. Her body jerked, but she managed to stifle her scream. She held as still as she could. She knew he was still there. His breathing was heavy and he wheezed every second or third breath.

Click. Click. Click. Click.

"Fuck," Luke yelled. He was out of bullets.

She heard the click-clack of his boots hitting the concrete. The sound faded. The car started again and moments later the sound of the engine faded into the distance.

She opened her eyes and saw that the chamber was lit. She turned slightly. The trap door was still open.

The sound of a car engine approaching roused Delilah from her sleep. The garage door banged its way open. She feared Luke had returned to finish her off. Delilah heard two sets of footsteps approaching. Thud-thud and click-clack echoed in the garage.

"Oh my God," a woman shrieked.

"What the hell?" a man asked. "Barbara, call nine-one-one. Now."

Delilah tried to speak but could only moan. She swallowed hard, clenched her fists, and reached deep down inside herself and managed a scream despite the burning throughout her body. The scream echoed in the cellar and throughout the garage above her. She stayed conscious long enough to see the couple staring down at her through the opening to the cellar. The looks on their faces were enough to tell her they weren't going to kill her. She smiled at them and then passed out.

###

"What the Sam hell?" Officer Marsh stared at the carnage spread out in the garage. On one side of the garage was the lifeless body of a man. On the other a woman slumped over in a chair with two bullet holes in her head. A little boy clung to her side.

"My God. What the fuck happened here?" Officer Spencer knelt next to the woman's lifeless body. The little boy wouldn't let go of the woman, his big blue eyes pleading for the policeman to save her. Spencer picked the boy up and held him on his hip, shielding him from the sight of the dead woman.

"I don't know. Call for back up, Spencer." In fifteen years on the force Marsh had never seen anything like this. He directed his attention to the man sitting in the corner. "You make the call to nine-one-one?"

The man nodded. "We live here during the winter months. We just got here today to find this... all these dead people." He pointed to the hole in the floor.

"Spencer, I'm going to check out whatever that is in the corner." Marsh walked over and was met at the cellar entrance by Spencer. The man sitting in the chair was pale and expressionless. His wife lie next to him, weeping in between bouts of vomiting.

"Ho-ly shit. Marsh, there's a woman down there."

Officer Marsh wanted to roll his eyes at his partner, but was too shocked. "Spencer, call for back up, the medical examiner, and get an ambulance." The portly cop climbed down the narrow wooden stairs. He sat down on the bottom step next. The young woman stared up at him. She was bruised and beaten. Her blond hair matted with blood. "You're going to be okay, miss. Everything is going to be okay."

The woman closed her eyes and smiled.

THE END

Made in the USA
Middletown, DE
15 September 2019